MICKY!

Charleston, SC
www.PalmettoPublishing.com

MICKY!

Copyright © 2022 by Katie Weaver

All rights reserved.

First Edition

Hardback ISBN: 979-8-8229-0482-8
Paperback ISBN: 979-8-8229-0483-5
eBook ISBN: 979-8-8229-0484-2

MICKY!

written and illustrated by
Katie Weaver

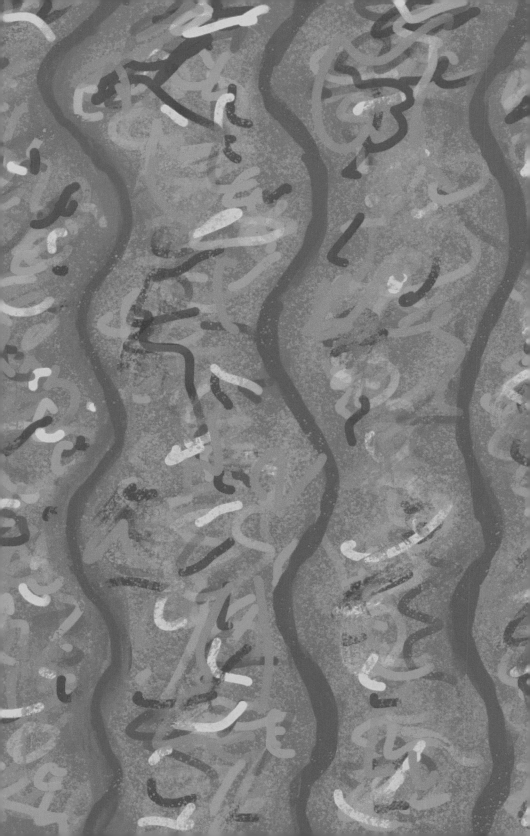

July 22nd
The day I brought
Micky home ♡

Flush! Flush!
What's that sound?

A world of wonder
is what Micky found.

A new water bowl,
just his size!

And a roll of white stuff,
what a prize!

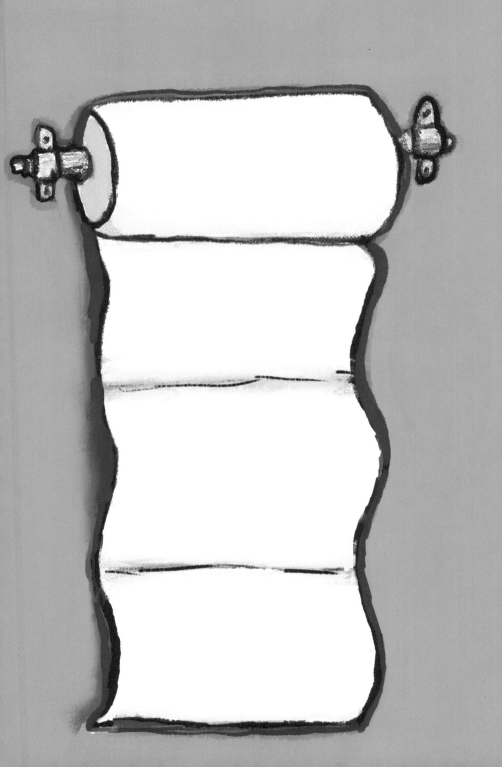

This shall be the
GREATEST DAY!

Until he heard a
loud voice say,

"Out you go!
Out you stay!"

"The bathroom is no place to play."

"I'm off to work.
I cannot stay.
Now be a good puppy
and behave!"

Well, Micky wandered around, feeling sad and bored,

until he saw
the open door.

This was his chance finally, at last, to unroll the toilet paper,

and eat the
TRASH!

He grabbed one end and
ran down the stairs.

Now there's
TOILET PAPER EVERYWHERE!

Micky jumped for joy at the mess he made

This was going to be an
AMAZING DAY!

BUT WAIT...

He heard a noise
and realized

that Julian was
still inside.

Julian heard a
THUMP!
A BOOM!
And a
CRASH!

"MICKY!
You better not
be eating the trash!"

But when Julian reached the stairs, what did he find?

TOILET PAPER EVERYWHERE!

"Look at this mess
all over the floor!"

"Katie must have forgotten to close the door."

"I won't bother to **SCREAM** or **SHOUT**, because very soon you will find out

that all the TRASH
you just ate is going
to give you one BAD
BELLYACHE!"

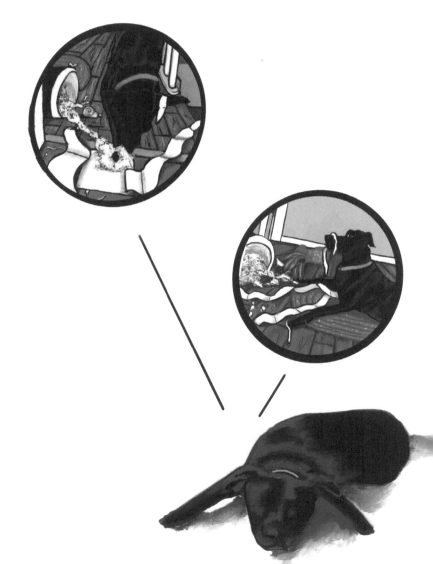

"Puppies make messes.
That's just what they do."

"Don't worry, Micky,
we still love you."

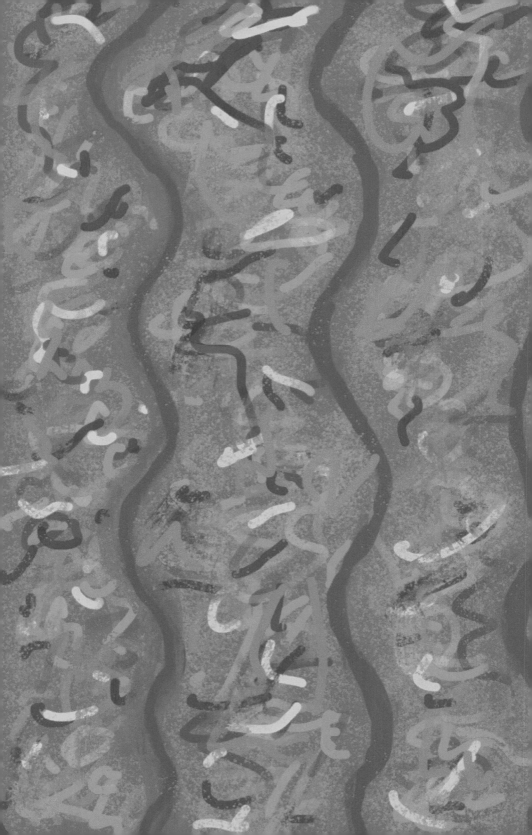

CPSIA information can be obtained
at www.ICGtesting.com
Printed in the USA
BVHW010336090223
658188BV00001B/2